To Pat B., Chris, Pat C., Laurie, Nancy, Laurence, and Linda—
amazing critique buddies, friends, and writers!
—C.P.

To all the little egg hunters out there.
—J.C.

HarperCollins Children's Books, a division of HarperCollins Publishers, 195 Broadway, New York, NY 10007
HarperCollins Publishers, Macken House, 39/40 Mayor Street Upper, Dublin 1, D01 C9W8, Ireland
Clarion Books is an imprint of HarperCollins Publishers.
Bunny in Disguise
Copyright © 2026 by HarperCollins Publishers
All rights reserved. Manufactured in Capriate San Gervasio, Italy.
No part of this book may be used or reproduced in any manner whatsoever without written
permission except in the case of brief quotations embodied in critical articles and reviews.
Without limiting the exclusive rights of any author, contributor, or the publisher of this publication, any
unauthorized use of this publication to train generative artificial intelligence (AI) technologies is expressly
prohibited. HarperCollins also exercises their rights under Article 4(3) of the Digital Single Market Directive
2019/790 and expressly reserves this publication from the text and data mining exception.
harpercollins.com

Library of Congress Control Number: 2025943420
ISBN 978-0-06-348303-3
The artist used Photoshop to create the digital illustrations for this book.
Typography by Rachel Zegar
25 26 27 28 29   RTLO   10 9 8 7 6 5 4 3 2 1

First Edition

BUNNY IN DISGUISE

By Cynthia Platt
Illustrated by Josh Cleland

CLARION BOOKS
An Imprint of HarperCollinsPublishers

Supermarket aisles bustling,
folks with shopping carts all hustling!
Who's that in the produce section
searching for carrot-y perfection?
Run right over, no delay!
The Easter Bunny's lost their way!

Egg hunt's starting at high noon!
That bunny has to hide eggs soon!

We must act now or they'll be late

for this important Easter date!

If the grown-ups see, they'll fuss and hover.

Let's get that bunny undercover.

Time to start off on our mission ...
bunny as a street musician!
Playing whistle, drum, guitar—
noisy notes that carry far.

Oops! A crowd has formed around—
this hop-star cannot be found!

Wait! Slow down and stop to talk
and to get some sidewalk chalk!
Find a route and a disguise—
gather round and strategize!

Have to help these eggs get hidden . . .

Take a stroll around the green . . .

with the cutest baby seen,

who never shows a hint of tears.

Don't fret—they'll grow into those ears!

Oh no! They've drawn another horde...
let's go back to the drawing board!

That's no bunny that you see.
It's springtime's finest bumblebee!

Rarest giant pollinator—
biggest north of the equator!
Flitting round on graceful wings—
just watch out for the giant stings!

And the bunny can't be found!

Problems? Two when there was one!
Easter Bunny's on the run!
Starting to get filled with fears.
Wait—do we see bunny ears?

Hurry up! The clock is ticking...

and a new idea is clicking!

What was that? That bird looks wrong?
They're part of the big turkey throng
that roams around the park each day
and gets in everybody's way.

That turkey is just like the group...
despite the pastel turkey poop!

Look! Here comes the big parade.

So much finery displayed!

Time to pull off one more caper.

Grab a bonnet—toilet paper!

Last disguise on Easter Day ...

to help the bunny get away!

Folks have gathered—celebration!
Egg hunt's held at this location!

Easter Bunny moving on.
Watch them hop across the lawn.
While the bunny's job is done . . .

we've missed out on egg hunt fun!

Look! There is one last surprise—
so good we can't believe our eyes.
Bunny magic for us all,
sweetest baskets by the wall.

Perfect treats on Easter Day...
because the bunny lost their way!